P9-DCV-573

BOOK CLUB EDITION

A FLY
WENT BY

by Mike McClintock

Illustrated by Fritz Siebel

Beginner Books

A DIVISION OF RANDOM HOUSE, INC.

For KIM and LESLIE

© Copyright, 1958, by Mike McClintock.

All rights reserved under International and Pan-American Copyright Conventions.
Published in New York by Beginner Books, Inc., and
simultaneously in Toronto, Canada,
by Random House of Canada, Limited.

Library of Congress Catalog Card Number: 58-9018.

Manufactured in the United States of America.

A   B   C   D   E   F   G   H   I   J   K
2   3   4

I sat by the lake.

I looked at the sky,

And as I looked,

A fly went by.

3

A fly went by.

He said, "Oh, dear!"

I saw him shake.

He shook with fear.

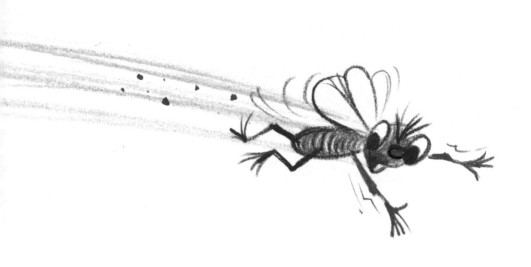

And when I saw that fly go past,

I asked him why he went so fast.

I asked him why he shook with fear.

I asked him why he said, "Oh, dear!"

He said, "I MUST GET OUT OF HERE!"

The fly said, "LOOK!

And you will see!

That frog!

That frog is after me!"

The fly went past!

The frog came ... FAST!

I asked the frog,

I asked him, "Why——?

WHY DO YOU WANT TO GET THAT FLY?"

The frog said, "Me?

I want no fly.

But I must hop,

And this is why . . ."

"That cat!" he said. "Just look and see!
That cat," he said, "is after me!"

Then he was gone
With one big hop.
The cat ran up,
And I said, "STOP!

Now, stop! Stop! Stop!" I told the cat.
"Do not pick on the frog like that!"

The cat said,

"Look, I want no frog.

I have to get away from . . .

SO . . .

The fly ran away
In fear of the frog,
Who ran from the cat,
Who ran from the dog.

One ran from the other.

The other ran, too,

From one who came after.

Now what could I do?

Away past the lake

Went the fly and the frog.

Away past the lake

Ran the cat and the dog.

They went past a shed,
And they went up a hill.
I ran!   And I said,
"I will stop them, I will!

The fly does not know that the frog is not mad.
The frog does not know that the cat is not bad.
The cat runs in fear of the dog, I can tell.
If I can stop HIM, then all will be well!"

I ran a lot.

I ran so fast,

I came up to the dog at last.

"Now, stop!" I said.

"You are the one

Who did all this!

Why do you run?

Why do you want to bite that cat?

Oh, you are bad to be like that!"

The dog said, "No! That is not so!

I want no cat.

The cat can go.

I do not want to bite the cat!

I run to get away from THAT!"

"That pig!" he said.

"Look back and see!

SHE likes to bite,

And she wants ME!"

SO . . .

The fly ran away
In fear of the frog,
Who ran from the cat,
Who ran from the dog.

The dog ran away
In fear of the pig.
My, she was mad!
And WAS she big!!

I said to the pig,

"So YOU are the one

In back of all this!

Now, why do you run?

Now, why should a pig bite a dog?" I said.

"And why are you mad?

Are you out of your head?"

The pig said, "I am NOT out of my head!
See what is after me! Look!" she said.

"That cow will hit me," said the pig.

"Those things up on her head are big!"

So the pig ran past.

She ran past . . . FAST!

Then the cow ran up,

And a little cow, too.

I said, "Now what got into you?

Do not pick on the pig, you two!"

The cow said, "Pig? The pig can go!

That is not why we run—oh, no!

But some one bad has made us run!

He wants to kill my Little One!"

I asked the cow,
"Who wants to kill
Your Little One?
Why, no one will!"

The cow said, "Look!
Up on the hill!
The fox is there!
He comes to kill!"

The cow and little cow ran past.

All full of fear they ran past

...FAST!

SO ...

The fly ran away
In fear of the frog,
Who ran from the cat,
Who ran from the dog.
The dog ran away
From the pig—and now
The pig ran away
In fear of the cow!

They came to the woods,

And there was a tent.

But they did not stop!

In and out they all went!

And last came the fox,

So HE was the one.

Who made them all fear,

And made them all run!

Yes, he was the one who was bad, I could tell.

If I could stop HIM, then all would be well!

I told the fox,

"Oh, shame on you!

Oh, shame, shame, shame

For what you do!

You want to kill the little cow!

You stop, or I will whip you—NOW!"

The fox said, "Now what did I do?

Why do you say, 'Oh, shame on you'?

I tell you I would never kill

That little cow!

I never will!"

The fox said, "This is why I ran——
Back in the woods I saw a man!
I saw a man!
He had a gun!

He wants to get me!
Let me run!"

SO . . .

The fly ran away
In fear of the frog,
Who ran from the cat,
Who ran from the dog.
The dog and the pig
And the cows—they all ran!
And then came the fox,
Who ran from the man!

They came to a house
And went down the hall.
And when they went out,
There was a big wall.
But that did not stop them.
Oh, no—not at all!

They ran and they ran.
They came to a town.
They went up one way,
And then they went down.

They went up one way,
And then down another.
They ran and they ran,
One after the other.

44

They came to a bank,
But they did not stop.
They went in the bank
With a jump and a hop!

With a jump and a hop
They ran in—and then
They went out the back way,
And ran on again!

I ran as fast
As I could run.
I told the man,
"YOU are the one
In back of this!
You are the one
Who wants the fox!
Put down your gun!"

"Fox? Fox?" the man said. "No!

I saw no fox,

But I must go!

For you should see,

Yes, you should see

The thing that now is after ME!"

"I did not see it," said the man.

"I took my gun and then I ran.

For I could hear it bump and thump

It was so bad it made me jump!

It was so bad it made me fear!

It was so big! It was so near!

It must be ten feet tall!" he said,

"And big and fat and bad and red!

Why, it can bite and kick and kill!

And it will do it! Yes, it will!

I hear it now! Come on, I say!

For I must run and get away!"

"BUMP!"
"THUMP!"

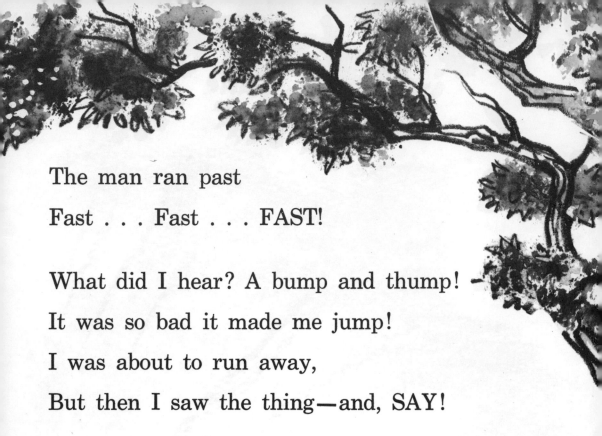

The man ran past

Fast . . . Fast . . . FAST!

What did I hear? A bump and thump!

It was so bad it made me jump!

I was about to run away,

But then I saw the thing—and, SAY!

It <u>was</u> not tall!

It <u>was</u> not mad!

It <u>was</u> not big!

It <u>was</u> not bad!

Was THIS the thing

That made them run,

And made them fear?

Was THIS the one?

It was a little sheep! So tame!

It came to me, and it was lame!

I saw what made the bump and thump.

I saw the thing that made me jump.

The sheep said, "Look at this tin can!

I can not get it off! I ran!

I ran for help! I saw a man.

I went to him, but then HE ran!

Why did he run away from me?

I just want help, as you can see."

I said, "I will get help for you!
And I can help the others, too!
For now I know just what to do!"

"Oh, man!" I called. "Come back! Come here!
This is a sheep, so have no fear!
The sheep wants help, for it is lame.
Come back! Come here!"

And then he came!

And then the man
Took off the can

56

But still the others ran and ran.

They did not know about the can.

I had to call so they would hear.

I had to tell them not to fear.

I had to tell them all was well.

And so I gave a great big yell . . .

I said to them all, "You must not run away!

No one is after you! No one, I say!

You all ran away—and now I know why.

I sat by the lake, and there came a fly.

The fly ran away
In fear of the frog,
Who ran from the cat,
Who ran from the dog.
The dog ran away
In fear of the pig,
Who ran from the cow.
She was so big!
The cow ran away
From the fox, who ran
As fast as he could
In fear of the man.
That man heard a thump,
And away he ran!
It was just a sheep,
With an old tin can!"

I looked at them all,
And then I could tell
They all had no fear,
And now all was well.

They all went away.

They all waved good by.

SO . . .

I sat by the lake
And looked at the sky.